Being Bella

• *Respecting Yourself* •

By T. M. Merk

Published by The Child's World®
1980 Lookout Drive • Mankato, MN 56003-1705
800-599-READ • www.childsworld.com

Photographs: Yuliya Evstratenko/Shutterstock.com,
cover, 1, 5, 19; 578foot/Shutterstock.com, 6; Julia Albul/
Shutterstock.com, 9; 3445128471/Shutterstock.com, 11;
SpeedKingz/Shutterstock, 13; BlurryMe/Shutterstock.com, 15;
LightField Studios/Shutterstock.com, 17
Icons: © Aridha Prassetya/Dreamstime, 3, 9, 11, 14, 17, 18, 22

ISBN HARDCOVER: 9781503827493
ISBN PAPERBACK: 9781622434398
LCCN: 2017961934

Printed in the United States of America
PA02379

About the Author

T.M. Merk is an elementary educator
with a master's degree in elementary
education from Lesley University in
Cambridge, Massachusetts. Drawing
on years of classroom experience, she
enjoys creating engaging educational
material that inspires students' passion
for learning. She lives in New Hampshire
with her husband and her dog, Finn.

Table of Contents

Being Bella

Bella did not want to do her homework.

"I just want to paint now," she said to herself. "I'll do my homework later."

When Bella went to her room to paint, Leo the paintbrush was waiting for her.

"Hi, Bella," he said. "It's time to brush up on **respect**."

"What do you mean?" asked Bella.

"Respecting yourself," Leo said. "Painting is fun, but homework is your **responsibility**. It helps you to practice what you learn at school. If you leave it for later, you might be too tired to do it or you might forget."

Learning is a great way to respect yourself! Learning helps you solve problems, help others, and discover people, places, ideas, and activities that interest you. You are never too young (or too old) to learn something new!

"I never thought of it that way," Bella said. "Are there other ways to respect myself?"

"Good question," Leo said. "Caring about your **hygiene** and **wellness** is part of respecting yourself too. Taking care of your health is important."

Hygiene is an important part of **self-respect**. It shows that you care about your health and appearance. Having good hygiene is part of wellness. Another part of wellness is having a healthy body weight and muscles! Doctors, dentists, nurses, and counselors help you to take care of your health. That means they help you respect yourself!

Bella wanted to know more. "When I **exercise** and eat well, does that show respect for me?" she asked.

"It does!" said Leo.

13

"And when I try my best and work hard?" Bella continued.

"Yes!" said Leo.

Anything you do to be a better you is self-respect! Working hard at sports, hobbies, and schoolwork is a way to show respect for yourself.

(7) $\dfrac{60}{11} = 5\dfrac{5}{11}$

(8) $\dfrac{73}{13} = 5\dfrac{8}{13}$

(9) $\dfrac{75}{15} = 5$

(10) $\dfrac{96}{17} = 5\dfrac{11}{17}$

(11) $\dfrac{100}{19} = 5\dfrac{5}{19}$

(12) $\dfrac{109}{21} = 5\dfrac{4}{21}$

Then Bella asked, "What if I show respect to someone else but that person is unkind to me?"

"You already know that you should treat other people with respect," Leo said. "But they should treat you with respect too. Standing up for yourself shows that you respect yourself. You should tell the person that he or she is being unkind."

If someone is unkind to you or someone else, tell that person that he or she is not being respectful. If the unkindness continues after that, be sure to tell a trusted adult. Repeated and purposeful unkindness is called bullying. Having self-respect means knowing that you deserve to be treated with respect!

"I see now that self-respect is good for me," Bella said. "It's time to start my homework!"

How is your self-esteem? **Self-esteem** is how much you respect and believe in yourself. The more you respect yourself, the more confident you will be!

Respectful Talk

Do you need help finding respectful words to say to yourself? Use these sentence starters to help with positive self-talk!

- This is hard for me now, but if I work hard I will do better with …

- _____ is good for me because …

- I believe in myself because …

- I don't need to listen to other people's negative words. I can use positive words like …

- I can always do better, so I will not give up on …

- I don't know this yet, but I will figure out how to …

S.T.E.A.M. Activity

Create Something to Wear

Directions: Create something to wear that reminds you to use positive self-talk. One idea might be to make a bracelet. Every bead can have a special meaning. You might touch the red bead to remind yourself not to give up. You might touch the blue bead to remind yourself that your health is important. Can you think of other ideas?

Time Constraints: You have 35 minutes to complete this project. Spend 5 minutes thinking about the positive self-talk that will help you and how your creation can remind you to respect yourself. In the next 10 minutes, plan how you will create your item. Are you making a hat, a bracelet, or a key chain? What is the best way to make your item? Gather all of the materials that you need, and then use the next 20 minutes to make your item.

Discussion: How do you feel when you speak respectfully to yourself? Does it help to make you feel better about yourself? Does it help to keep worries away? What else can you create for yourself?

Suggested Materials:

- Beads
- Cloth
- Glue
- Markers
- Paper bags
- Pipe cleaners
- Safety scissors
- String

Glossary

exercise: (EK-ser-syz) Exercise is movements that increase your heart rate.

hygiene: (HY-jeen) Your hygiene is how clean your body is.

respect: (rih-SPEKT) To respect is to show that you care about a person, place, thing, or idea.

responsibility: (reh-spon-suh-BIL-uh-tee) When you are expected to do something, it is your responsibility.

self-esteem: (SELF uh-STEEM) Your self-esteem is how you feel about yourself.

self-respect: (SELF rih-SPEKT) Self-respect is caring about yourself.

wellness: (WELL-ness) Your wellness is how healthy your body is.

To Learn More

Books

Dismondy, Maria. *Spaghetti in a Hot Dog Bun: Having the Courage to Be Who You Are.* Wixom, MI: Cardinal Rule Press, 2008.

Montague, Brad. *Kid President's Guide to Being Awesome.* New York, NY: HarperCollins Children's Books, 2016.

Pett, Mark. *The Girl Who Never Made Mistakes.* Naperville, IL: Sourcebooks Jabberwocky, 2011.

Web Sites

Visit our Web site for links about respecting yourself:
childsworld.com/links

Note to Parents, Teachers, and Librarians: We routinely verify our Web links to make sure they are safe and active sites. So encourage your readers to check them out!

Index